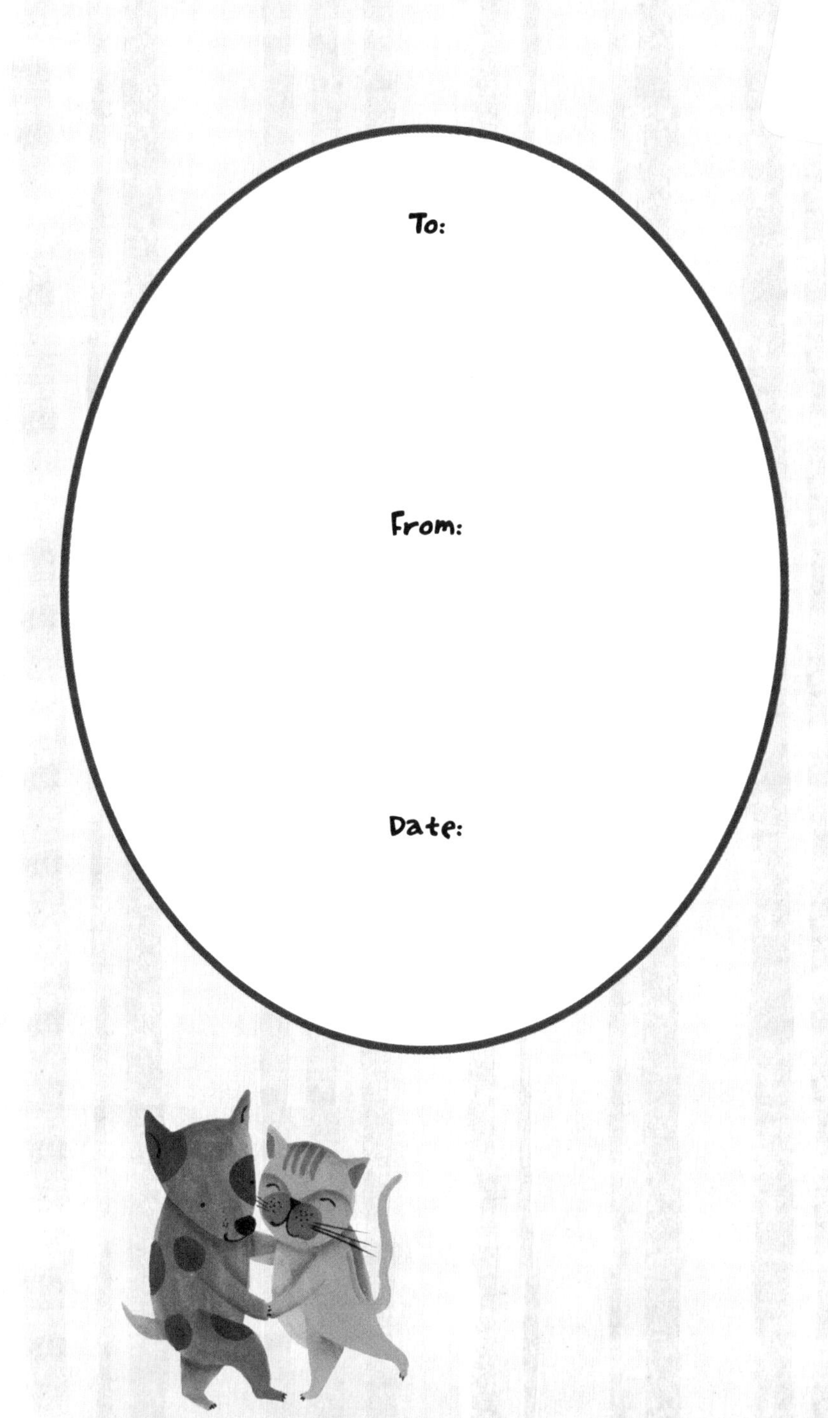

To:

From:

Date:

What Will I Be When I Grow Up?

How God Made Me Somebody Special

Written by Susan Snyder

Illustrated by Valeria Cis

HARVEST HOUSE PUBLISHERS
EUGENE, OREGON

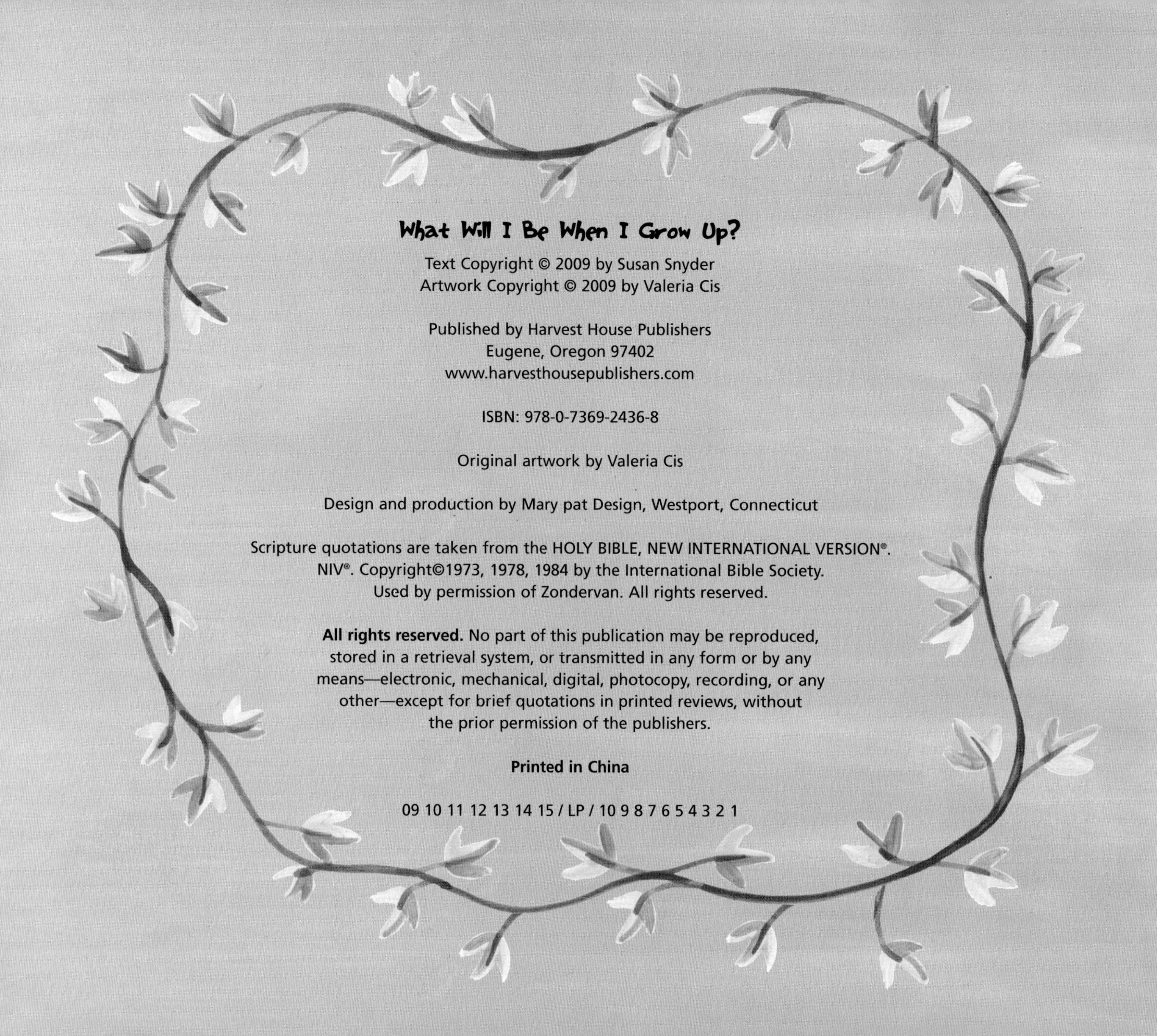

What Will I Be When I Grow Up?

Published by Harvest House Publishers
Eugene, Oregon 97402
www.harvesthousepublishers.com

ISBN: 978-0-7369-2436-8

Original artwork by Valeria Cis

Design and production by Mary pat Design, Westport, Connecticut

Printed in China

09 10 11 12 13 14 15 / LP / 10 9 8 7 6 5 4 3 2 1

This book is lovingly dedicated to my precious daughter, Ashley.
It is my fervent prayer that God will bless you with a deep
desire to please Him each day of your life. I love you dearly.
Your mom, Susan Snyder

Para Facundo, Olivia, Ignacio, Victoria, y Tomás,
por lo que deseen ser cuando sean grandes.
(For Facundo, Olivia, Ignacio, Victoria, and Tomás, for what they would like to be when they grow up.)
Valeria Cis

Sometimes I sit around and wonder,

"What will I be when I grow up?"

Will I be a doctor or a nurse...
and give people medicine to make them feel better?

Maybe, but even if I'm not...I can cheerfully give others the good news that God's Word is the best medicine for a troubled heart.

"A cheerful heart is good medicine." Proverbs 17:22

Will I be a teacher...

and teach children exciting lessons in a classroom?

"Be kind to everyone, able to teach." Timothy 2:24

Will I be a recording artist...
and sing for lots and lots of people?

"I will sing of the Lord's great love forever;
with my mouth I will make Your faithfulness known." Psalm 89:1

Will I be a police officer...

and stop people from fighting and hurting each other?

Maybe, but even if I'm not...I can be a peacemaker and share God's love with people who are hurting.

"There is...joy for those who promote peace." Proverbs 12:20

Will I be a travel agent...

and arrange vacations for people to fun and exciting places?

Maybe, but even if I'm not...I can tell people the gospel story so that they can go to the most wonderful place of all—heaven!

"God so loved the world that he gave his one and only Son, that whoever believes in him shall not perish but have eternal life." John 3:16

Will I be an author...

and write interesting stories for children to read?

Maybe, but even if I'm not...I can write notes and cards and send them to people to cheer them up.

"Encourage one another daily." Hebrews 3:13

Will I be a farmer...

and grow food to feed people all around the world?

"Jesus declared, 'I am the bread of life. He who comes to me will never go hungry, and he who believes in me will never be thirsty.'" John 6:35

Will I be a Hairstylist...
and help people to look beautiful?

Maybe, but even if I'm not...I can live my life like Jesus and be beautiful on the inside, always showing God's love to others, and celebrating the inward beauty of others.

"Your beauty...should be that of your inner self, the unfading beauty of a gentle and quiet spirit, which is of great worth in God's sight." 1 Peter 3:3=4

Will I be a builder...

and construct comfortable homes for families to live in?

Maybe, but even if I'm not...I can build my life on God and His truths which last forever and help build the faith of others.

"Dear friends, build yourselves up in your most holy faith and pray in the Holy Spirit." Jude 1:20

There are many, many different things

that I might be when I grow up...

But what I really want to do is please God in EVERYTHING I do!

I know that whatever I do, God will help me live my life to please Him every day!

Whatever you do,
work at it
with all your heart,
as working for
the Lord.
Colossians 3:23